ELLA
Diaries

TOP
SECRET!

With thanks to Gemma Dean-Furlong and the Gold Street Clifton Hill PS Reading Club M.C.

Meredith Costain

For Jade, Zoe and Ray. I love our Saturday morning Breakfast & Ballet days. x D.M.

Danielle McDonald

Scholastic Australia
345 Pacific Highway Lindfield NSW 2070
An imprint of Scholastic Australia Pty Limited
PO Box 579 Gosford NSW 2250
ABN 11 000 614 577
www.scholastic.com.au

Part of the Scholastic Group
Sydney • Auckland • New York • Toronto • London • Mexico City • New Delhi • Hong Kong • Buenos Aires • Puerto Rico

Published by Scholastic Australia in 2015.

National Library of Australia Cataloguing-in-Publication entry

Author: Costain, Meredith
Title: Ballet backflip / Meredith Costain; Danielle McDonald, illustrator.
ISBN: 978-93-5275-639-1
Target Audience: For primary school age.
Subjects: Diaries--Juvenile fiction.
Schools--Juvenile fiction.
Other Authors/Contributors: McDonald, Danielle, illustrator.
Dewey Number: A823.3

Typeset in Sweetie Pie.

First edition : January 2019
This edition :March 2020

Printed in india at Ram Printograph, Delhi

ELLA Diaries

Ballet Backflip

Saturday, before dinner

Dear Diary,

You will never ever EVER believe what happened today!

I was at ballet class like I normally am every Saturday morning. My ballet class is held at:

(which is just a fancy way of saying Mrs Fry's ballet school). Except, actually, the school isn't very fancy at all.

The main reason for this is because ballet is held in our local scout hall. Which means when we're not there, the scouts are. Which is a VERY BAD THING.

Reasons why Sharing YOUR SPACE with SCOUTS is BAD:

1. Scouts are (mostly) boys.

2. Boys often SMELL BAD (especially when they have been running around playing sweaty scouty games. Ewwww.)

3. Boys leave old bits of chewy under the seats.

4. They also leave BOY GERMS all over the wooden barre we hold onto when we are doing our *demi-pliés*. (Which is another fancy word for a type of knee-bending exercise.)

So anyway, we were all in the middle of our warm-up stretches when Mrs (I mean Madame) Fry announced that she had an important announcement to make. Of course we all wanted to know **IMMEDIATELY** what the important announcement was going to be. But Madame Fry said we had to wait until the end of class. And that she would only tell us if we had all worked really hard with

NO SLACKING OFF.

So then we had to finish off our warm-up stretching, do all the knee-bendy *plié* things at the *barre*, and practise all our leaps and jumps and twirls across the floor (my favourite part) before we could find out. Mrs Radinsky (who is about 896 years old) played tinkly music on the piano (which is even older) while Madame Fry walked around the room putting our legs and arms in the right place or checking to see our backs were straight and our bottoms tucked in.

Sticking your bottom out in ballet is the **WORST THING YOU CAN POSSIBLY DO.**

Then she said we had to wait until we'd completed our warm-down stretches before she revealed her important announcement. By then of course everyone was getting really twitchy, busting to know what it was. There was Madame Fry telling us to be **CALM, CALM, CALM**, when actually we were all **CRAZY, CRAZY, CRAZY**, buzzing like little ballet bees trapped in a bottle. Especially Zoe and me. We **LOVE** important announcements (especially if they have anything to do with chocolate cake.)

Then, finally, we stretched our last stretch and it was time! Madame Fry turned to us, her eyes shining like twin twinkly stars, and said:

'Everyone, I have something VERY VERY exciting to tell you.'

We all turned to each other, our eyes shining like ~~76~~ ~~92~~ a sky full of twinkly stars, wondering what the exciting thing might be.

Possible EXCITING things MADAME was about TO TELL US:

1. Our *École du Ballet* has been discovered by a famous movie producer, and we are all about to become famous movie stars.

2. A pop star wants us all to appear as dancers in his next video clip.

3. Mrs Radinsky is going to retire.

4. A ballet shoe company has decided to award us all ~~$500~~ $10,000 dance scholarships and give us ballet shoes for ever and ever.

5. An advertising company needs two **brilliant dancers** who look just like Zoe and me to appear in a TV commercial for chocolate cake.

And then Madame Fry said, 'Girls and boy,* we're going to . . .'

Oops! Sorry, Diary, Mum's calling me. I'll have to tell you what Madame actually said when I get back from dinner.

* This is **NOT** a mistake, as there really is only one boy at our *École du Ballet*. His name is Don Tay. Well, that's what Zoe and I call him anyway, even though we accidentally discovered one day while reading a list of names on the noticeboard that it's actually spelt like this:

Oops! Guess he's lucky his last name is Biggins and not Tay (like Daisy Tay) or he'd be Don Tay Tay. ☺

Saturday night, after dinner

Back again! So, Madame Fry's BIG announcement. Well, I can officially tell you it was NONE of the possible things on my list. No movie deals or video clips. Or scholarships. Or TV ads for chocolate cake. ☹

Instead, her big announcement was that we are going to be doing a 'dance play' she has written herself called *The Enchanted Woods* for our ballet recital this year. We all have

to dress up as bunnies and pixies and mushrooms and babyish things like that.

All the little kids in the junior class started squealing and clapping their hands and dancing round in circles saying things like, 'Ooo, I want to be a bunny, with a fluffy tail. **PLEEEEASE**, Madame! Can I **PLEASE** be a cute little bunny?'

But the kids from the senior class, like me and Zoe and Daisy Tay, just stared at each other **IN HORROR**.

I used to love our ballet recitals. We'd dress up like real, professional dancers in stylish floaty costumes and wear cool make-up and perform beautiful leaps and twirls.

But dancing mushrooms? Bleuchhh.

Then Madame Fry told us something else. Something that **IS** more exciting. She needs two dancers from the senior class to be the **Fairy King** and **Fairy Queen**. They will be doing a special dance together called a *pas de deux* (which means 'dance for two people' in French. You say it like this: pah de der).

It's pretty obvious who the Fairy King is going to be, isn't it?

You got it. Don Tay.

It's so not fair. Even if he was the ~~worserest~~ badderest dancer in the whole *École du Ballet*, Don Tay would still get the part. And believe me, he is **NOT VERY GOOD**.

But **EVERYONE ELSE** in the senior class is going to want to be the Fairy Queen, so they can wear a floaty dress instead of a mushroom or fluffy bunny outfit (even if it means we have to do a pas de deux with Don Tay). I can't believe this is happening!

That's it for now, Diary. See you tomorrow.

Sunday night, before bed

Dearest Diary,

Zoe came over today for an emergency meeting about Madame Fry's *The Enchanted Woods* announcement. We put a sign up on my bedroom door that said:

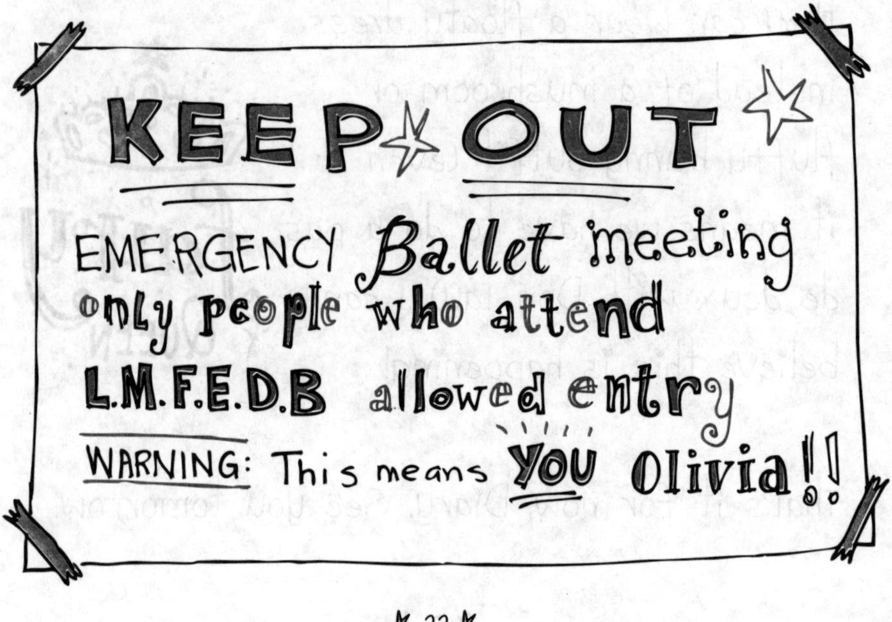

* L.M.F.E.D.B. stands for La Madame Fry École du Ballet.

** Olivia is my little sister who likes to poke her nose into everything, especially stuff that is NOHB (none of her business), which is most of the time.

We need a PLAN. Zoe thought we should try writing a petition, like we did when we had The Great Seat Swap Crisis on the first day of school. But we couldn't think of anything to put in it that would make Madame Fry change the dance play to something else. (Something more 'ballet-ish'

and less woodsy.) Not when all the junior kids thought it was such a FABULOUSLY FABULOUS idea. And especially not when it was something she had written herself ☹

So then we thought the best thing to do was make sure one of us got the Fairy Queen part. After that, we could try to convince Madame Fry to give her a Fairy Queen Assistant or a Lady Butterfly-in-waiting. (Some kind of stylish part that also needs a floaty dress).

YESSS! That should do it.

We finished off our meeting with some extra ballet practice, so Madame Fry will see we are the best dancers to play the Fairy Queen and her Butterfly-in-waiting.

Then, when Zoe left, I wrote a shape poem* about ballet and pinned it to my noticeboard.

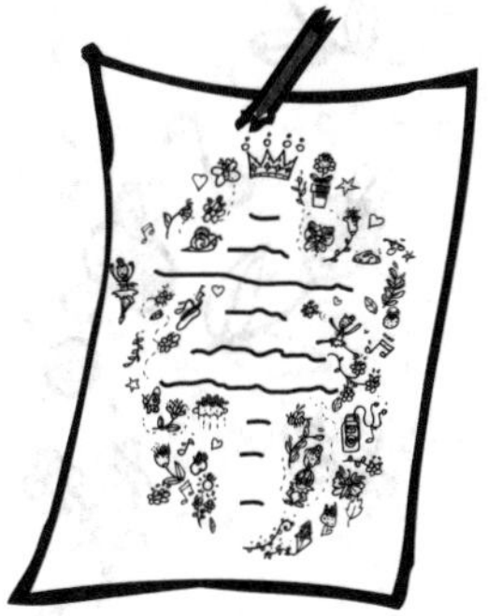

I
am a
jumping
whirling
twisting
twirling
ballerina
All day long I spin and leap, floating across the room
like a
graceful
butterfly
I point my feet
and extend my arms
making pretty patterns
on the floor and in the air
I stretch my leg out behind me
and hold it there while I count to ten
one
two
three
four
five
six
seven
eight
nine
ten
I am a
dancer!

Madame Fry has to choose me to be the Fairy Queen. She just HAS to!

* Shape poems are poems where the words make the shape of what you are describing. My excellent and exceptionally talented teacher Ms Weiss showed us how to write them. They are also called concrete poems, though I am not 100% sure why—I've never actually seen any poems written in concrete.

Monday, after school

Hello, Dearest Diary,

Can you believe this??? Zoe and I were in the girls' toilets* at lunchtime when we heard Fifi and Jazmin come in.

*Zoe and I are BFFs to the power of 10, which means we do lots of things together, like having sleepovers, wearing identical stylish outfits, and needing to go to the toilet at exactly the same time.

We couldn't see them because we were both inside cubicles with the doors shut but we could hear everything they said. Their conversation went like this:

Fifi: Madame Fry is SO going to choose me to be the Fairy Queen.
Jazmin: No way.
Fifi: Yes way. I'm the best dancer.

Jazmin (laughing like a maniac): Ha ha ha ha ha.

Fifi: OK then. Name one person better than me at dancing.

Jazmin: Me.

Fifi: Oh, yeah. OK then. Name two.

Jazmin: Easy. Esther. Also, Maddy G, Daisy, Ariel, Kitty, Zoe, Chelsea, Maddy M, Cordelia, Grace, Rani, Ella and Don Tay.

Fifi: What!!! NO WAY are any of those better than me. Especially Don Tay. Eww.

Then their voices trailed off as they went outside. Zoe and I opened our cubicle doors at EXACTLY the same time and came back out to where the basins are. Then we looked at each other and laughed like hyenas at what they'd been saying. Fifi and Jaz might THINK they are good dancers but WE KNOW BETTER

But the whole time I was laughing I was ~~sekr~~ secretly worrying about something Jazmin said. It was the place she put me in the list of dancers who are better than Fifi. Second last! And only one place ahead of Don Tay, who, as I've previously told you, is NOT the best dancer in the world. She even put me behind Grace (who is the type of dancer who ALWAYS has her bottom stuck out, no matter how many times Madame Fry tells her to tuck it in.)

NOOOOOOOOOOO!

What if everyone at our *École du Ballet* thinks that I'm a hopeless dancer too? Especially Madame Fry!

I'm going to practise really, really hard in my room every day until I get good enough for her to choose me to be the Fairy Queen.

Catch you later, DD.

Tuesday, before bed

Hey there, Diary,

As soon as I got home from school I pushed all the furniture in my bedroom against the walls so I'd have lots of space to practise my dance steps. I did lots of *pliés*

and jetés

and battement tendus

and relevés.

Then Mum said I had to take Bob for a walk. I kept right on practising my ballet steps while I was walking him.

It was fun! (Though I got some VERY strange looks from other dog-walkers, especially as I was wearing a tutu.)

Good night, Diary. Sleep tight!

* Ballet steps always have fancy French names. Madame Fry says this is because ballet started in France. I reckon it would be really cool to invent your own style of dancing and make up the names for the different steps. You could have things like the Ella Boogaloolella or the Zoe Uponmytoesies.

Wednesday, after dinner

Dear Diary,

Today, when I was practising my *battement tendus* in my room so my legs and feet and toes will be nice and strong for when I do jumps and toe rises, Olivia and her friend Matilda barged in even though I had my

sign on the door. They kept making fun of me by saying silly immature little girl things like, 'Look, Ella. We're being bee-yootiful ballerinas just like you,' and, 'Look at me, I'm a ballet STARRR,' while they flopped and flounced around the room, then collapsed into giggles on my bed.

And when I told them to leave Olivia went tattle-taling to Mum (in that high, whiny voice she puts on when she wants something): 'Mu-um! Ella's being MEAN.'

So then Mum gave me one of her famous lectures about how I should be nice to my dear, sweet, darling little sister, who I am lucky to have. (Not!) Then she made me teach Olivia and Matilda some easy-peasy dance steps, like first and second position. Bleuchhh. These steps are so basic even the teeny tiny little beginner ballet kids can do them with their eyes shut.

I should have been working on much trickier and highly-demanding steps to demonstrate my technical superiority at ballet class on Saturday.

Even though I didn't really mind teaching them in the end, it is still SO NOT FAIR!!! I am angry to the power of 100,000.

(Sisters are The Worst!!)

Thursday, after school

Dear Diary,

Today was really rainy and stormy. The sky was filled with lightning flashes and thunder crashes.

So Zoe and I hung out in the undercover area at lunchtime instead of playing B-Ball (which is our name for basketball) like we usually do.

This would have been perfectly fine except for one thing. My ex-BFF Precious Princess Peach Parker was there too, sitting at a bench right next to us.

EX-BFF → Peach Parker

This meant we had to listen to Peach and her friends Prinny and Jade talking to each other in EXTREMELY LOUD VOICES about how fantabulously fabulously fabulous they are. Then Peach got down on the floor on her tummy and bent from the middle so that her feet were touching the back of her head.

Of course then all the other girls had to come over and say things like, 'Wow, Peach, that's aMAZing!' and, 'You're so flexible, Peach, I wish I could do that,' and other sickeningly sick-making stuff. (I mean, I'm pretty flexible too, after all those hundreds of hours of warm-ups we do for ballet, but you don't see me showing off in front of practically the whole school like that.)

Then Prinny whispered something to Peach and she jumped up and started doing backflips on the same spot. One after the other. Over and over and over. Then she started again. Only she did something she called roundoffs this time, which looked a bit like a cool cartwheel.

By now a big group of kids had come over to watch. Peach finished up with one last flip. Then she gave everyone a really fake modest* smile like it was no big deal that she was so naturally talented and went and sat down on the bench again with her copycat friends.

*Modest means the opposite of BIG SHOWOFF—but she doesn't fool me one little bit.

Zoe turned to me, her eyes shining like shiny eyes. 'Zow-ee,' she said. 'I wonder where she learnt how to do THAT.'

'Do what?' I said, pretending to yawn. 'That boring thing she did with her feet or the flippy things?'

'All of it,' said Zoe dreamily. Her eyes were now so shiny I could see my reflection in them. And I didn't look happy. 'Backflips look like way more fun than the steps we do in ballet.'

What was she saying? Ballet is **BEAUTIFUL!** And a lot of the stuff we do—like leaps and jumps and *arabesques* and *pirouettes*—is just as amazing as backflips done over and over on the same spot.

I looked over to the B-Ball courts. The storm had stopped storming and the sky was clear again. I grabbed Zoe's hand.

'Come on,' I told her. 'It's stopped raining. Let's go and finish off our B-Ball game.' But all the time I was running up and down the court after the ball, I kept thinking about the backflips Peach had done, how they did look kind of fun, and wondering if they were something I could do too.

Have to stop writing now. Mum wants me to play with Max for a bit as she has an important deadline** tomorrow and he keeps on interrupting her by trying to show her his bug collection. Catch you later, Diary!

** Mum is a graphic designer. She designs lots of really, really important stuff, like things for TV and magazines.

Friday night, after dinner

Hey there, Diary-O,

Here are some interesting things I found out today:

1 The place Peach and her friends go to learn gymnastics is called Twisters. It's a big, shiny new building at the back of the SupaValu Store. I can't believe I've never noticed it before.

2 They've been going there for MONTHS.

3 Her gymnastics class is on Wednesdays (after school) and Saturday mornings (at the same time as my ballet class).

4 Five girls from Grade 5 are going to start going to Twisters, after watching Peach's display in the undercover area yesterday.

I have to go now.
Last chance for ballet practice! Wish me luck for tomorrow.
XOXOXOXOXOXOXOXOXOXO

Saturday, before lunch

Dearest Diary,

I can't write anything right now. I'm too ~~distrort~~ distraught.*

*Distraught means sad, to the power of 10 gatrillion. Imagine how you would feel if you really liked something (like chocolate cake) and you were just about to eat a ginormous piece of it, and then someone threw it under a bus and it got all squished, with dirt all

mixed in with the icing and even some dead bugs (crunchy ones) as well. That's how I feel right now.

Saturday afternoon, I am not 100% sure of the time and who cares anyway, my life is over

Hello Diary,

OK, I'll tell you what happened. But WARNING: This is a very, very, very sad story. You may need tissues. ☹☹☹

I arrived at ballet class feeling really confident after all my practice during the week, dressed in the most stylish outfit I could put together from what was in my wardrobe (and with a little bit of help from my Nanna Kate, who used to be a style queen herself when she was young (back in the Dark Ages)). I was thinking about borrowing one of Olivia's fairy wands to add to the 'look' but decided against this at the last moment as I didn't want to show up the other girls in the class too much.

Long Gloves
Flower Garland
PINK Ribbon Belt
Sparkly tights
LOTS OF TULLE

I did my warm-up stretches extra carefully and made sure my bottom was tucked in while I was doing my *barre* exercises, especially when Madame Fry was walking past.

And when we did the leaping and jumping steps across the floor, I kept repeating these words in my head:

I am the Fairy Queen.
I am the Fairy Queen.
I am the Fairy Queen.
I am the Fairy Queen.
I am the Fairy Queen.

Over and over, so that my leaps would be

L O N G E R

and my jumps

H
I
G
H
E
R

and my arms more fluttery and graceful and elegant.

Then Madame Fry clapped her hands and asked us all to sit down on the floor in front of her. Everyone stopped their leaping and jumping and elegant arm-fluttering and raced over. We all sat down with our legs daintily crossed and our hands politely clasped in front of us and looked up at her expectantly.* Zoe and I gave each other a smiley wink for good luck, though of course we didn't really need it.

* This means having an excited feeling that something thrilling or interesting is about to happen. For example, my little brother Max kept looking **expectantly** at Bob, our golden retriever, because he thought Bob was going to have puppies, like Molly, the dog from next door, who got really big and round just before she had them. When in actual fact Bob was just fat because of all his midnight raids on our pantry.

Madame Fry began by telling us all how lucky we were to be dancing in this exciting new performance. And then she let us know which parts we'd all be playing. As she read out each group of names there were excited squeals (mainly from the little kids) as they discovered whether they were going to be bunnies, baby deer, frogs (bleuchhh), blackbirds or magical trees.

And then she spoke the WORDS OF DOOM that changed my life forever.

'The names of the talented students who will be playing the Fairy King and Queen are . . .'

(everyone in the senior class looked up at her hopefully)

'Don Tay Biggins'
(no surprises there)

'and . . .'

(I held my breath, waiting for my name to roll off her lips)

'Esther Grech!'

NOOOOOOOOOOOOOOOOOOOO!

I turned to Zoe, my face a mixture of shock, horror, amazement, astonishment, ~~incradool~~ incredulity and disbelief. 'B-but . . .' I stammered, so overwhelmed by all those things I just wrote about I could barely speak. Then I pulled myself together enough to whisper, 'Esther can't be the Fairy Queen. She just can't. And what are we going to be? Madame didn't say our names.'

And then I had a thought. Maybe there were two new parts EVEN BETTER than the Fairy Queen, written especially for us, Madame Fry's best and most reliable dancers. Parts where we could jump and leap and soar across the stage like prima ballerinas.

But, according to Zoe, she'd said our names all right. I just hadn't heard them over all the squeals of excitement coming from the fluffy bunny brigade.

Zoe was going to be a frog.

And me?

I was going to be a magical rock.

Saturday night, very late, so late even Mum and Dad have gone to bed. I know this because I can hear Dad snoring through the wall

How could Madame DO this to me, Diary?

Saturday night, even later

Rocks don't even dance. They just sit there, looking rock-like.

Sunday, middle of the afternoon

Sorry, can't tell you anything right now, Diary.

I'm too busy sitting here really, really still, practising my ROCK dance.

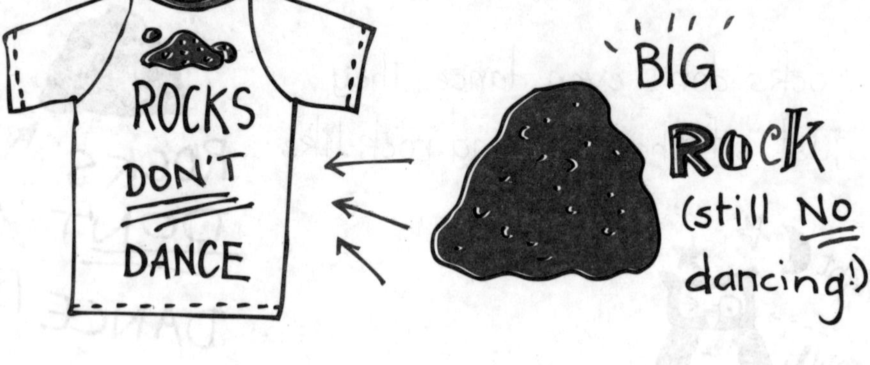

Monday, before bed

Madame Fry is a great big meanie
Stopped me from being the Fairy Queen(ie)
Now I'm feeling sad and glum
Being a rock is just plain dumb.

Wednesday, after dinner

Dearest Diary,

Today has *not* been a good day. ☹☹☹

Firstly, Olivia has been in my room again. She must have snuck in while I was helping

Mum get dinner ready.

I know this because:

1. My room smells like that awful pretend lip gloss that she and her friend Matilda put on each other when they're playing dress-ups.

2. Stuff on my desk has been picked up and put down again in a slightly different place.

3. Some of the clothes hangers in my wardrobe are facing in a different direction.

(4) One of my books, *My Best Book About Ballet*, has been taken out of my bookcase and put back in the wrong place. (Next to *Become a Style Queen in 46 Simple Steps*, which is **COMPLETELY** the wrong section for it to be in.)

I was just about to dob on her to Mum when Dad poked his head around my door. (Hasn't he ever heard of **KNOCKING??!!**)

'Zoe's on the phone for you, Ell Pell,' he said, handing it to me. (I HATE it when he calls me that.)

As soon as Dad had left my room and I was sure he was out of hearing range, I whispered (just in case he wasn't), 'Hi, Zo. It's me.'

'Guess what!!!' Zoe practically screamed at me.

I thought hard. 'Madame Fry has changed her mind and made me the Fairy Queen after all?'

'Nope,' trilled Zoe. 'I went to Twisters!'

And then she told me the whole story. About how upset she was at having to be a frog. And how she kept thinking how fabulous Peach's backflips were. And how she'd convinced her mum to let her try a gym class to see if she liked it.

'It was EXCELLENT,' she insisted. 'And FUN. You would LOVE it. I'm going back on Saturday morning. Come with me, Ell. Ple-e-ease?'

I reminded her that Saturday morning was our ballet class with Madame Fry so how could I possibly go? Besides which, I was **COUNTING** on her being there to help me get through the shock of having to learn my boring rock dance while Esther Grech skipped around with a big fat smirk on her face doing a pas de deux with Don Tay.

Then Zoe reminded *me* that none of this sounded like it was going to be excellent **OR** fun. And that she was **ADAMANT*** that she would be going to Twisters again instead. And if I didn't want to come with her then I wasn't a very good friend.

And then *I* said that if she didn't come with me to ballet then *she* wasn't a very good friend.

* Adamant means that you have made up your mind about something and no-one can talk you out of it **NO MATTER WHAT**. (It is also the name of a very nice, friendly ant I used to have when I was ~~seven~~ ~~six~~

younger. I kept Adamant in a shoebox with Petronius, my pet praying mantis, but he didn't stay in there for very long. I am not 100% sure if this is because he escaped or if Petronius ate him. ☹)

After that there wasn't much left to say. So we both hung up.

WAAAAAAHHHHHH!

Thursday morning, before school

Nothing to say.

Thursday afternoon, after school

Still nothing.

Friday, before bed

Once I had a friend called Zoe
We did everything as one
Now she'd rather twist and tumble
She says ballet is no fun.

Saturday afternoon, snuggled up under my doona

Hello Diary,

So this morning I went to ballet class.

I kept the space beside me free during warm-up stretches and at the *barre* in case Zoe stopped being adamant about going to Twisters and decided to come with *me*—her true and eternally BFF and ballet buddy—instead. But she didn't turn up.

By the time we'd finished our floor routines, I knew for sure she wasn't coming. I had to tough it out all on my own.

Four of us are doing the rock dance: me, Grace (the bottom sticker-outer), Fifi and Daisy. Madame Fry taught us the steps. Most of it was pretty easy. There are lots of *sautés* (jumping up and down steps), and also steps where you spring from one foot to the other, called *petit jetés*, which we did while holding hands with our arms crossed across our bodies like the dancers in *Swan Lake*. These were kind of fun, especially when Grace and I kept stepping on each other's toes while we were learning how to do them.

I was starting to think being a rock wasn't so bad after all—until I saw the designs for our costumes.

They are UGLY, UGLY, UGLY, UGLY!!

Every time I think about them I feel like crying. ☹☹☹

And then something really, really strange happened. Madame Fry asked me if I could help her teach some steps to the little ones.

Me.

The girl she chose to be a rock.

But she said she chose me because she thinks that I am 'very responsible' and would make a good teacher. She wants Zoe to help too (for the same reason) but I had to tell her that I'm not 100% sure that Zoe is coming back. Ever. (My voice kind of choked up a bit as I was saying that but I'm not sure she noticed.)

So now, not only do I have to do the Dance of the Rocks *without* Zoe, I also have to teach 25 excited squealing little girls with sticky hands and bad posture the Dance of the Fluffy Bunnies. Without Zoe.

It's going to be

HORRERRIFUL!*

* 'Horrerriful' is a word I made up that means a mix of horrible, terrible and awful, to the power of 100.

Saturday night, in bed

Hey Diary,

You know when things get so bad you think you're going to explode into a million bits and float around in the universe for ever and ever and ever?

And then something else even ~~badder~~ worser happens, and there aren't words horrerriful enough to describe it.

At dinner, I was telling Mum and Dad about how Madame Fry has asked me to help her teach the Ballet Bubs to do the bunny dance, because she thought I was 'responsible'. (Mum and Dad LOVE to hear things like that.)

And then Olivia looked at me with this big goofy grin on her face and said, 'Hey, Ella! You could try out your teaching on MATILDA AND ME FIRST! It would be FUN!'

Mum said what an excellent idea that was and that we could all start tomorrow. And—horror of horrors—she needed lots of quiet time because she has another deadline so we had to do it IN MY BEDROOM!!!

Both of them. Olivia AND Matilda. Flouncing around being bunnies in my bedroom, where I keep all my most precious things. (Like you . . . *sssshhhhhh.*)

Why, Diary? Why?

Sunday, before bed

Dear Diary,

There was only one person who could help me get through this terrible day.

Zoe. 

Getting her to come over was going to be kind of hard though, given we haven't spoken since we hung up on each other four days, two hours, 32 minutes and ~~16~~ ~~15~~ 14 seconds ago (not that I'm counting or anything). NOT EVEN at school!

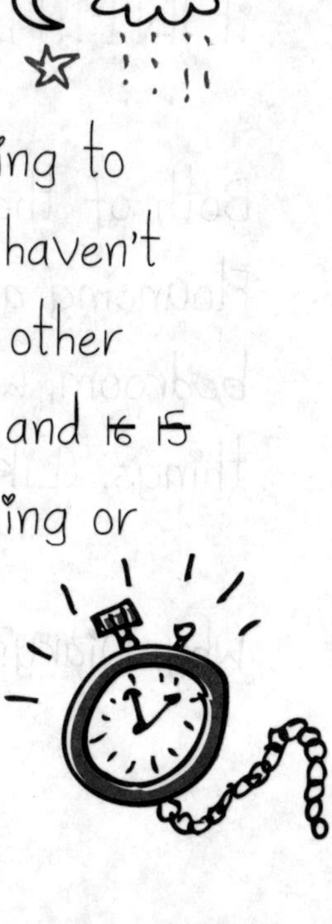

I crossed all my fingers and toes, then called her.

This is how our conversation went:

Me: Hello?

Zoe: Who's speaking please?

Me: It's me.

Zoe: I'm sorry. I don't think I know you.

(I **KNEW** she was going to make it hard for me.)

Me: It's Ella.

Zoe: Ella? The mean Ella who doesn't want to come to Twisters with me and have fun?

(That is SO NOT FAIR!!
I ALWAYS want to have fun!)

Me: No. Ella, your best friend who desperately needs you to help her out today or she will die a slow agonising death of distress, distraughtness and destruction.

Zoe: Seriously? What's happened?!

Phew! Zoe was finally talking to me again!

I explained about how Mum was making me teach Olivia and Matilda the bunny dance in my room, and what a horrerriful time I was already having and that if she didn't come over to help me I would DIE. Tragically.

And Zoe stopped being adamant about never talking to me again unless I went to Twisters with her and agreed to come over to help me out.

Which just goes to show you that she is A TRUE FRIEND.

All this writing is VERY EXHAUSTERATING, dear Diary, so I'm going to have to stop now and write the rest tomorrow.

Good night
Sleep tight
It's no fun when
Best friends fight ☹

Monday morning, still in bed, just before I have to get up for school

Good morning, dearest Diary!

So, things got MUCH CHEERIER AND BETTERER when Zoe came over to help me out. We taught Olivia and Matilda how to do pliés,

and *pirouettes*,

and *arabesques*,

and how to skip around the room and waggle their tails like the fluffy bunnies will do in *The Enchanted Woods*.

It was ~~acksh~~ actually kind of fun (though I would **NEVER EVER** let Olivia know this), even though it was a bit squeezy with us all in my bedroom.

After we'd finished our ballet lesson, we went out into the backyard and Zoe showed us some of the things she's learnt to do at Twisters.

She did headstands and handstands up against a tree.

Then she did cartwheels from one end of the yard to the other, finishing with her legs together in a roundoff. She told us her group is going to start learning how to do backflips soon too.

I **REALLY, REALLY, REALLY** want to learn how to do that kind of stuff—it's **aMAZing!** SO much better than a boring old rock dance. Flipping your body upside down then over like that looks kind of scary, but if I practised really hard I'm sure I could do it too. I just have to find a way . . .

Monday, after school

Dearest Diary,

Now that lots of kids are going to Twisters it looks like the new craze at school is going to be gymnastics. Daisy told us our sports teacher, Mrs Finfinger, was starting up a gymnastics club at lunchtimes in the gym. So we decided to check it out!

We peered through a window into the gym to see what was going on inside. Mrs Finfinger had set up the tumbling mats and Prinny and Jade were showing everyone how to do supported handstands that dropped down into forward rolls. (Then some of the other kids tried, but theirs were **REALLY BAD**, with arms and legs sticking out all over the place instead of being neatly tucked in, like they were octopus rolls.)

Peach was walking along a balance beam and then she did what looked EXACTLY LIKE AN ARABESQUE!!! The same kind of *arabesque* I've been doing FOR YEARS at our *École du Ballet*!

Zoe zoomed into the gym, dragging me with her. 'Come on, Ella,' she whispered. 'If Peach can do it, we can do it. Only better.'

But there's a **BIG** difference between standing on one leg with your other leg sticking high into the air when you're on a nice, safe flat floor, and doing this move standing on a teeny tiny narrow little plank of wood.

I looked at Peach, now doing split jumps and cartwheels along the beam, and then I looked back at Zoe again.

'You mean do an *arabesque* UP THERE? On the BEAM?'

Zoe nodded. 'I tried it on Saturday. Not the cartwheels. I can't do them yet on the beam. But I did an *arabesque* on it, and other leg-extendy things. Ella, it was aMAZing! And there's lots of other moves they do at gym which are just like ballet steps. Only they're 100% more fun!'

Peach had finished on the beam and was now doing walkovers and those fun-looking backflips on the floor mat again.

And that's when I made up my mind. No way was I going to be a silly magical rock when I could do something really cool instead. I'm going to stop ballet classes, and start learning gymnastics instead.

Monday, before dinner

There is just one teensy tiny problem. Convincing Mum to let me change.

But I have A PLAN.

Wish me luck, dear Diary.

Monday, after dinner

Sadly, things did not go well with my plan.

Here is a small part of what happened.
Scene: The dinner table, which I have

thoughtfully set with the best plates and some mixed flowers from the garden in Mum's favourite vase.

Me: Mum?

Mum: Yes, Ella.

Me: The logo for that new website you've been working on looks REALLY good.

Mum (sounding pleased): Thank you, Ella.

Me: You're **REALLY** good at designing things.

Mum (glowing): Thank you, sweetheart.

Me: I think it's really important to only do stuff you **REALLY**, **REALLY** like doing, don't you?

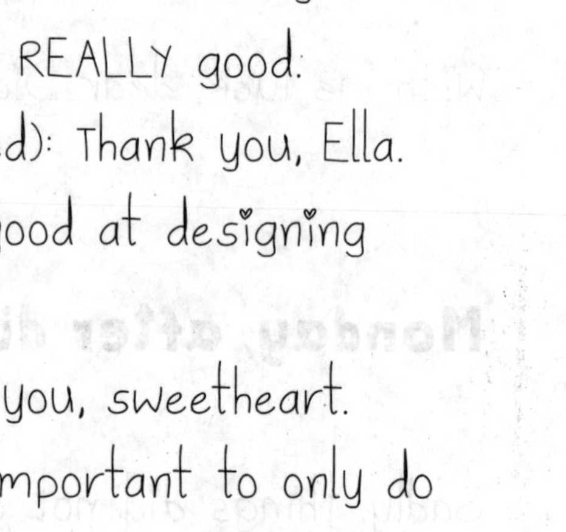

Mum (looking a bit suspicious): Er . . . yes?

Me (mumbling this bit really quietly, in the hope that Mum doesn't actually hear what I'm saying, and just says, 'Yes, dear' to be polite. And then I will change the topic to something else immediately, like the weather in ~~Ooz~~ Uzbekistan or the price of apples or something):

Wchmmmdnballetmnnnwwwm ngymchnnnmmmwwnmnd.

Dad: Speak up, Ell Pell, we can't hear you.

Mum: And stop mumbling please.

Me (in a slightly louder voice

and not mumbling): which is why I want to stop doing ballet and change to gymnastics instead.

Mum and Dad (together):

I'm not going to put the rest of what they said here, dear Diary, because I am too distraught (again), and also my arm is getting tired from writing all this down.

But the short version is:

No, you can't.

Monday, about an hour later (though it's hard to judge time ~~acku~~ accurately when your dreams have been stomped on by a close relative)

I am feeling a bit better now so will write more about our ~~conf~~ ~~conva~~ what happened at dinner. Although I am not 100% sure my arm is strong enough yet to write it all down so I will do it in point form, like my excellent teacher Ms Weiss ~~tort~~ taught us to do when we are planning our school projects.

Reasons why MUM AND DAD (But mostly MUM) won't LET ME CHANGE FROM Ballet TO GYMNASTICS:

★ ~~Because they are mean.~~

♡ Because they think I want to change just because Zoe did. (OK, this bit is partly true.)

✿ Because Mum says she knows how much I really love ballet and I'm just cross right now because of the rock dance crisis and I will regret* dropping it later. (Also partly true.)

Because Mum says she has recently paid out 'good money' for a new ballet uniform and she doesn't like seeing it go to waste.

Because Mum says I have already made 'a commitment'** to Madame Fry to help her teach the Ballet Bubs and I should never back down from commitments, especially seeing as how I am so 'responsible'. (OK, I set myself up for that one.)

It's not looking good, Diary, but I will **NEVER GIVE UP** on my quest to become a brilliant gymnast like Peach.

* 'Regret' is what you have when you do something you shouldn't have and then realise it was a **BIG MISTAKE**. Like when our dog Bob jumped up and ate **ALL** of the cookies Mum had just made for our school fête, and had a tummy ache and stinky bottom for days. I bet he **REALLY** 'regrets' that.

** A commitment is when you promise you will do something—cross your heart, hope to die. Like when Zoe and I made a commitment to each other to be best friends forever, even if one of us had to move to an extremely faraway place, like the other side of the railway line.

Monday, about two hours later

I just asked Mum again and she sighed and said, 'Go to bed, Ella, we'll discuss it in the morning.'

Do you think this means she's changed her mind?????

Tuesday morning, before school

I just asked Mum again. The answer is still no.

Tuesday morning, just before I walked out the door to go to school

Still no.

Tuesday morning, just after I came back in again, pretending that I had forgotten my poetry folder

Still no.

Tuesday afternoon, about five minutes after I walked in the front door carrying a bunch of mixed flowers I picked from Mr Supramaniam's garden (only the ones that were sticking through the fence into 'shared public space', so it doesn't count as stealing)

Still no. But I think she might be cracking, just a teeny tiny bit.

Tuesday night, really, really late

I got out of bed to get a drink of water and when I was accidentally on purpose ~~sneaking~~ walking past the lounge room where Mum and Dad were watching TV I heard them say my name and then these words:

Do you think this means they're going to let me go?????

Wednesday morning, before school

Mum says I can go to Twisters with Zoe!!!! But only on a trial basis (which I found out means just this once and if I—or Mum and Dad—decide it's not 100% the right thing for me then I have to go back to ballet for ever and ever).

And if I want to still do gym after the trial lesson, I have to keep going to ballet school on Saturday mornings until the ballet recital is over, to keep my 'commitment' to Madame Fry to teach the Ballet Bubs the bunny dance.

And I have to wear my ballet outfit to gym class, even if other girls think I am the daggy one in the pale pink leotard and flesh-coloured tights when they are wearing super-stylish aqua/lime green/hot pink/midnight blue* lycra leotards with contrasting panels and matching hair ties.

But who cares? **I AM GOING TO TWISTERS!**

* pick one

Wednesday night, just before lights out

Dear darlingest Diary,

I went to Twisters! And it was aMAZing!!! So different from ballet school.

Ways TWISTERS is DIFFERENT from L.M.F.E.D.B.

TWISTERS	L.M.F.E.D.B
♥ Gleaming NEW building where everything is new and shiny	☆ Stinky old scout hall with boy germs and pre-chewed chewies under the seats

Funky young instructors you can call by their first names who have amazing flexibility and teach cool techniques like backflips	Madame Fry who has been teaching the same steps since around the time of the dinosaurs (the really ancient ones)
LOUD music from big speakers that makes you want to MOVE, MOVE, MOVE	Tinkly piano music from Mrs Radinsky that makes you want to fall asleep Zzzzzzzzzzz
Totally awesome equipment like the balance beam and springboard	NO equipment, unless you count the boring wooden *barre* (which I don't)

And guess what? (You'll never be able to, Diary, because you weren't there, so I'll just tell you.)

You're allowed to stick your bottom out. In fact they positively **ENCOURAGE** it. Grace would **LOVE** this place!!

Zoe took me over to the warm-up area where everyone was doing their stretches. Which is just like what we do at ballet class!

And then we did some exercises that strengthen your legs and arms so you'll be able to do all the gym moves properly. Which is also just like we do at ballet class!

Matty (who is our instructor) told me my stretches and exercises were really good for a beginner. And then he asked me if I'd ever done ballet. I could see Peach was listening in with this really snooty, unmodest look on her face. So I told Matty, 'No. I'm just **naturally talented**.'

(But then when Peach walked away, I explained I was only joking.)

Ha! That will teach old Princess Peach not to mess with **ME**.

But the best thing about gym class was the leaps and jumps. In ballet class, when we do *grand jetés*, we have to leap up high using just our bodies. But in gym, we have a springboard to help us. I could leap **HIGHER** and travel **FURTHER** and stay in the air for **LONGER**. It was

Zoe was right. Ballet is good and everything, but gym is excellent. And definitely **MORE** FUN!

I am **ABSOLUTELY POSITIVELY TOTALLY** coming back next week.

Saturday afternoon

Dearest, bestest Diary,

I'm sorry I haven't written in you for a few days, but I've been **BUSY, BUSY, BUSY**.

Now that I have passed Mum and Dad's 'trial basis' test, they have agreed that I can keep going to Twisters on Wednesdays with Zoe.

YAY! Even if I do have to wear my pink ballet leotard. I guess it's not too bad, especially after Nanna Kate helped me to jazz it up a bit with some sparkly blue sequins and a purple zigzaggy flash across the left shoulder. It's gone from plain, plain, plain to Zow-ee!

Every day after school I do TWO lots of exercises. My ballet stretches AND my gym stretches. I am going to be so stretchy and flexible. Nanna Kate says they will soon start calling me **THE HUMAN RUBBER BAND**.

Then, after that, I give Olivia and Matilda a quick ballet lesson in my room.

Because guess what? Over these past two weeks I have discovered three things:

1. Olivia and Matilda are actually pretty good at ballet. In fact, they started at Madame Fry's *École du Ballet* today! And because they already know all the steps, they are going to be fluffy bunnies in *The Enchanted Woods* ballet recital next weekend!

2. I enjoyed teaching them. That's right. I know it's hard to believe. Me, Ella. Enjoying hanging out with her little sister, Olivia, the snoop of the century. (Just don't ever tell her. And if she *does* say something about it, I will **KNOW FOR SURE** she has been

snooping around in my room reading you.)

3. And guess what else? I've also enjoyed helping Madame Fry teach the Ballet Bubs. They all look so cute in their teeny tiny little pink leotards and frilly tutus and when they come up to give me big squeezy hugs or hold my hand I don't even mind (even though their hands are usually **REALLY** sticky. Bleuchhh.)

Have to go now, Diary. Zoe's coming over soon to show me what I missed out on this morning and we're going to practise together. Our group is starting backflips at Twisters next week and I have to be ready—I CAN'T WAIT!

Catch you later, dear Diary.

PS (one week later)

I've just got home from *The Enchanted Woods* ballet recital.

It was aMAZing!

Mum and Dad bought tickets for themselves and Max and Nanna Kate. But because I was on the program as an official helper, I got in for free. And we all got to sit in the **FRONT ROW!**

Madame Fry and some of the parents who like doing art had spent ~~hours~~ minutes decorating the stage so that it looked just like a real enchanted forest, with cut out trees with wavy branches that reached out like witchy hands and paper flowers and toadstools stuck to the back wall with staplers and a giant cardboard moon shining in the giant cardboard sky.

The first dancers to come out on the stage were my **Ballet Bubs** doing the **Dance of the Bunnies**. They all looked so sweet (even Olivia), waggling their little fluffy tails (even though two of them forgot their steps and just wandered aimlessly around the stage for a while).

I felt really, really proud, like I was their mum or something.

And then Grace and Fifi and Daisy and Cordelia (who took my place when I dropped out) came on to do the Dance of the Rocks. They were really funny and everyone laughed. (Although I'm not 100% sure that it was actually supposed to be a comedy number. Oh well.)

But what everyone was REALLY waiting to see were the stars of the show, Esther and Don Tay, doing their pas de deux. Madame Fry must have been giving Don Tay private lessons or something because he was actually dancing really well.

Until the bit where he had to pick Esther up and twirl her around.

And he got tangled up in her floaty dress.

And dropped her.

And she had to go to hospital in an ~~amber~~ ambulance.

Whew.
That could have been me. I *knew* there was a good reason to change from ballet to gym! ☺

XOXOXOXOXOXOXOXO

PPS (two weeks later)

In case you were wondering, Esther is OK. Mostly. She has a BIG bruise on her hip where she landed on the floor, and a broken toe. Everyone wanted to sign her cast. And she got lots of cards and flowers, just like Madame Fry did at the end of the recital.

I made Madame Fry this card to say thank you for being such a good ballet teacher.

Madame Fry
You are so sweet
You have tiny
Ballet feet
Thanks for making
Lessons fun
You'll always be
My Number One!

Love Ella xxx

I'm not 100% sure yet, but if I get time, I'd like to keep helping her to teach the little kids. But I'm DEFINITELY going to keep going to Twisters. I love gymnastics—especially when I get to do it with my BFF!

See you soon, Diary. I'm off to practise my backflips in the backyard with Zoe. Then we're going to eat chocolate cake and watch this video Matty lent her about famous gymnasts in the Olympic Games. He reckons we can both start training for gym comps soon. Who knows? We might end up in the Olympic Games ourselves!!!

Love Ella xox

Chocolate
CAKE
ME
1

Write your own **shape poem** inside this frame:

This time, create your own shape poem and decorate it any way you like!

You can read all about Ella in her other diaries:

It's a new school year, and it's perfect. Until class starts that is, and EVERYTHING goes wrong. Ella can't believe that her absolutely WORST ENEMY EVER, Peach, is sitting next to her! No matter how far Ella moves her new pencil case across the desk, Peach is IN HER SPACE. Where's her BFF Zoe? How can this year get ANY WORSE?

Ella and Zoe want to start their own dog walking business. They make a sign, hang it up in shops and wait by the phone for their first call. When their only job turns out to be minding a lizard, and then **SNEAKY** Peach Parker starts behaving **VERY SUSPICIOUSLY**, Ella starts to wonder what's up. Zoe and Ella must go **UNDERCOVER!** With their detective notebooks (and outfits) in hand, can Ella and Zoe uncover the **TERRIBLE TRUTH?**

ELLA Diaries

Read more of Ella's brilliant diary in

Double Dare You

I ♥ Pets

Dreams come true

Christmas CHAOS

and look out for more coming soon!